The Fabulous Cakes of Zinnia Jakes

The Crumbling Castle

For Bingley and Bess, my own magical cats.

NEW FRONTIER PUBLISHING

First published in Great Britain in 2020
by New Frontier Publishing Europe Ltd.,
Uncommon, 126 New King's Road, London SW6 4LZ

www.newfrontierpublishing.co.uk

ISBN: 978-1-912858-48-4

Illustrated by Nancy Leschnikoff
Text copyright © Brenda Gurr, 2020
Illustrations copyright © New Frontier Publishing, 2020

Edited by Stephanie Stahl
Designed by Rachel Lawston

A CIP catalogue record for this book
is available from the British Library.

Printed and bound in China

The paper and board used in this book
are made from wood from responsible sources.

1 3 5 7 9 10 8 6 4 2

The Fabulous Cakes of Zinnia Jakes

The Crumbling Castle

Brenda Gurr

Chapter 1

The best cakes I've ever eaten! They must be the work of The Genius Chef.

Magical! Is this some type of witchcraft?

Her cakes are out of this world! But please answer me this. Who is Zinnia Jakes???

'Zoe! Pay attention!'

Zoe slammed shut her ScreenTouch and tried to slide it under her spelling book. But it was too late! Miss Wagner's beady eyes were extremely sharp. She was already swooping down.

'Is that a ScreenTouch?' she asked, thrusting out her hand. She made it sound like something that tasted disgusting.

Zoe shook her head, then gave up and handed it over. Miss Wagner flipped open the cover and tapped the screen with a tangerine fingernail. She peered at it.

'This is supposed to be a maths lesson, Zoe. Look at fairy cakes in your own time!'

The kids in the row behind Zoe laughed. One kicked her chair. She didn't even have to turn to see who it was. It was *always* Lucas. He'd called her 'Freckle Face' on her very first day of school and had been annoying her ever since.

Miss Wagner was taking the ScreenTouch back to her desk. 'Besides,' she said, 'cakes are full of sugar and very bad for you!'

Zoe said nothing. She happened to know that her teacher had a Zinnia Jakes cake box in the staffroom fridge. It had been delivered for Miss Wagner's birthday that very morning. Her sister had ordered her two pink fairy cupcakes at 6.46 p.m. the day before. Zoe knew this because Zinnia Jakes was not a TV chef, nor a witch, nor even the world's greatest magician. Zinnia Jakes was a nine-year-old girl. Zinnia Jakes was Zoe Jones.

Zoe only realised she had a talent for baking two years ago, on her Aunty Jam's birthday. On that day, she'd woken up with a picture in her mind as clear as shards of sugar glass. She would make a surprise birthday cake for her aunt. She'd just read a book about exotic birds so it had seemed a good idea to make a cake in the shape of an emu. The legs and neck were made of chocolate mousse and the rest had been a beautiful rich hazelnut sponge cake. Zoe had barred her aunt from the kitchen and spent all morning on it, even ruffling up the icing to make it look like shaggy feathers. Jam had almost tripped over her music stand when Zoe had brought out the cake. And when her aunt had tasted it, she'd reached out for Zoe's hand and said it was the most glorious cake she'd ever eaten – as delicious as any of Zoe's mum's creations.

Zoe had wished her mum was still alive to hear that. Violette Picard had been one of the most famous pastry chefs in the world.

Then Jam's fork had clattered onto her plate. She'd had a fabulous idea: Zoe could start her very own cake-making business!

Right away, Zoe had frowned. 'But who would buy cakes from a kid?'

'We won't tell anyone who you are,' said Aunty Jam. Her hand had strayed to the hot-pink flower in Zoe's hair, a zinnia, freshly picked that morning. Jam had waved it like a magic wand. 'We'll sprinkle the business with mystery … you can have a secret identity!'

'Like Dad?' Zoe felt fizzy bubbles rising

in her stomach from excitement. Her dad's job as an international food writer was top secret. He had to visit restaurants all over the world to taste and write about the food – usually in disguise. He'd fallen in love with Zoe's mum in a restaurant in Paris after she'd presented him with one of her extraordinary desserts.

Jam had laughed. 'Yes. Like your dad. Or a spy … one who works undercover to bake and deliver cakes. Let's do it, Zoe! First, we need a name for you and your fabulous cakes, something with a lovely rhythm …' She'd stared at the zinnia in her hand and snapped her fingers. 'I've got it!'

And that was how Zinnia Jakes had burst into life.

Zoe smiled to herself and spun her pencil between her freckled fingers. She still felt butterflies in her stomach when she thought about her baking adventures.

Then she realised Miss Wagner was glaring at her and she quickly bent over her work.

When the home-time siren went, Zoe went straight to Miss Wagner's desk.

Miss Wagner rapped her fingers on the ScreenTouch. 'Zoe, this is just not good enough ...'

The same words as always. Zoe tried not to yawn. She pretended to listen to Miss Wagner's stale lecture. Then she took the ScreenTouch, yanked up her jellybean socks, grabbed her bag and charged straight out to see her best friend, Addie. She was practising handstands in the playground in her usual spot. Even though plenty of kids were pushing past her, she still managed to keep her balance. She was a superstar!

Zoe waited for Addie to turn back up the right way. She thought about her baking schedule. Miss Wagner's cakes had marked the end of a busy two weeks. *What would turn up next?* She sighed. There were only so many teddy-bear and fairy cakes one could make without getting bored. She hoped a new challenge wasn't far away!

Chapter 2

'Did you get it back?' asked Addie, still upside down.

Zoe patted her bag and nodded. 'Luckily.' She leaned against the sun-warmed wall, scuffing her glittery sneakers on the path. 'Have you got gym today?'

Addie flipped gracefully onto her feet. Her cheeks were raspberry red. 'Yes. I've got extra coaching this week. Our class is practising for a tumbling act that we are performing at the medieval fair this weekend.'

'Really?' Zoe pictured Addie doing

precise cartwheels in front of a cheering crowd. She'd only ever seen one of Addie's gymnastics displays last year, when she'd delivered a farewell cake for Addie's coach. Addie had helped to smuggle the cake into the girls' locker room, fitting in her mission between the uneven bars and balance beam events. She'd managed everything perfectly, of course. 'That's great! I'll be there too!' Zoe continued. 'Jam and Ben will be playing medieval music.'

'That's so cool!' said Addie. 'I like it when they play together. Ben's an awesome guitarist!'

Zoe nodded. She felt glad that Jam had formed a music duo with Ben, her old university friend. In the past year, Ben had become a good friend to Zoe too.

'I also want to enter the competition,' said Addie, stretching up high.

'What competition?' asked Zoe.

She peeled off her grey school jumper. Her favourite cherry-cupcake shirt was underneath.

'Zoe!' Addie sighed. 'Miss Wagner was just telling us about it. It's being run by the maths teachers from Mount Rumbling School. You have to design and make a model catapult from recycled things.'

'You're going to be great at that,' said Zoe. 'Lots of calculating and measuring and—'

Pat-a-cake, pat-a-cake … Music wafted out of Zoe's bag.

The girls froze. Zoe whipped her head around to make sure no-one was listening. But it was way too noisy in the playground for anyone to have noticed.

'It might be an order,' Addie whispered. 'Quick, have a look!'

Zoe pulled out the ScreenTouch and a message popped up.

Hi Zinnia Jakes!

I'm a medieval history professor and I'm launching my latest book at the Mount Rumbling fair on Sunday. I know it's late notice, but I would love to order an authentic medieval cake to display at my stall. Could you make it a crumbling castle? Thank you,

Nina

'Wow!' Addie clapped Zoe on the back. 'Can you do it? It's Friday already.'

Zoe felt a wiggle of excitement. 'A crumbling castle cake? This is perfect!'

She closed her eyes for a moment. She could picture a battered old castle, perhaps made out of chocolate, on a grassy marzipan hill. It had towers and ... what were those round bits on top of a castle's roof called? Turrets?

'Well, let me know if I can help,'

said Addie. 'You'll need a lot of precise measurements to make a strong castle.'

'Yeah, thanks, Ads!' said Zoe.

Addie looked up. 'Oh, there's my mum. I've got to get to gym. See you later!' She scooped up her bag and sprang off towards the school gate.

Zoe watched as Addie jumped into her mum's car. Then she stood still for a moment to allow the castle she was dreaming up to set more firmly in her mind. It would look great as a cake! She grabbed the ScreenTouch and her jumper and shoved them into her bag. She raced across the playground and darted through a knot of chattering kids and parents. She couldn't wait to get home!

Chapter 3

Zoe's feet whizzed over the ground towards her street. It was only a two-minute walk from school but somehow she still managed to be late every now and then! She kept thinking about the new cake and was starting to see an even clearer picture of a crumbling castle in her head. Now a drawbridge and a murky moat were appearing too. She hugged herself with excitement.

Zoe was so busy with her ideas that she almost ran straight past home. She grinned to herself, slid to a stop and then turned into the driveway. Staring at the gravel underfoot, she added that idea to her castle picture as well – a stone pathway leading up to the cake would look excellent. Plus she'd always wanted to use those coloured chocolate rocks from the sweetshop in town. They would be perfect!

Zoe crunched her way towards the front door of Jam's cottage where she stayed every time her dad went off on his secret food missions. Aunty Jam was really Jamie, but no-one ever called her that.

Ben's tiny black car was parked just behind Jam's blue and green van, named Beethoven. Beethoven transported all the things Jam and Ben needed for their music performances. It also doubled as a top-secret cake delivery vehicle for Zoe's spectacular creations! Zoe patted Beethoven's dented front door as she went past. He hadn't been running so well lately. But Jam said they had to wait until she was paid for her next performance before they could fix him.

Zoe went up the wooden front steps, expertly avoiding the jagged splinters, and pushed hard on the front door. As it squeaked open, she breathed in a minty scent. It reminded Zoe of candy canes and made her mouth water. Jam must have lit a peppermint candle.

'Hi, sweetheart!' Jam was sitting in the lounge room on the chair with the lumpy cushion. But she still looked elegant, like fine lace on a wedding cake. Her dark hair trailed down one shoulder. She waved her cello bow and blew a kiss. 'How was school?'

'Okay,' said Zoe, smiling at Ben, who was sitting cross-legged on the sofa and arranging his music sheets. He grinned back and nodded. He was balancing a strange instrument in his lap. It was like a small stretched guitar. 'How's the practice going?'

Jam glanced at Ben and wrinkled her nose. 'It's difficult!'

'Yeah, we're playing these medieval instruments instead of cello and guitar,' said Ben.

Zoe looked over at the wall. Jam's precious cello was on its stand.

'Should we run through the music again before your students arrive?' asked Ben.

'Yes, we've probably got time,' said Jam.

'If it doesn't take too long, I can take a peek at Beethoven before I go,' said Ben, looking out of the window. 'But I really think he needs a mechanic.'

'Don't worry,' said Jam. 'Beethoven hasn't let us down yet!' She leaned over and picked up another strange instrument from under her chair. It looked a bit like a flat cello.

Jam held it out to show Zoe. 'This is a vielle. Ben's is called a citole. We're borrowing them from the university for the special medieval fair this weekend.'

'They're super cool,' said Zoe, her eyes running over the gleaming satin wood. 'I bet people will love them.'

'Would you like to hear us play?' said Jam.

'Sure, but maybe later on,' said Zoe. She hopped on the spot like popcorn in a pan. 'I have to plan something.'

'I've made strawberry pancakes for your snack. They're on the kitchen table,' said Jam, with a smile. 'Oh, and Coco's waiting for you. I think she might be bored.' As she said it, a yowl came from the back of the house.

Zoe laughed. 'Thanks, Aunty Jam. I'll go and see her.'

Chapter 4

Zoe dropped her bag and dashed down the hallway with the ScreenTouch in her hand. She glanced back. Ben's head was bent over the citole, so it was safe. She sometimes wished that Ben knew about Zinnia Jakes but Jam said they had to draw the line somewhere. Ben didn't need to know, she said, and the fewer people who knew the better.

Zoe ducked into the kitchen. She swallowed down two pancakes as fast as possible (yum!). Then she headed towards the old crème caramel rug on the wall that her dad had brought back from his travels. Zoe pulled one of its ragged corners aside to reveal a narrow, hidden archway. She stepped forward onto the chequered tiles and sighed. Instantly, bright colours seemed to glow and warm her face. The Zinnia Jakes kitchen was her favourite place in the entire world!

She was so lucky that Jam had set it up for her. It felt like being in the middle of a giant fruit salad, with multi-coloured cupboard doors circling the room and a long orange bench covered in tins jammed with cookery tools and gadgets. A huge walk-in pantry took up one corner, with bulk supplies of things like sugar, honey and spices. There was also a shiny oven and a stovetop, both nearly new. Zoe loved it all.

Coco the cat was in her usual position, high up on the wooden bookcase filled with Zoe's recipe books and folders.

She meowed and gazed at Zoe with her golden eyes.

Coco had mysteriously arrived on Jam's doorstep three years ago at midnight. Her demanding yowls had pierced the night air until Jam had grumpily opened the door. Coco had sauntered in, placed herself on the rug and stretched out her legs one at a time. After Jam had fed her some chicken, that was that – Coco had made herself at home. And although Jam had asked around, no-one seemed to be missing a cat. Zoe was very happy about that because the moment she'd met Coco they'd become instant friends.

Zoe assumed that Coco's life before she'd moved in must have been interesting because she had so many un-catlike skills. This seemed to include an extensive knowledge of baking. With a flick of her tail or a loud purr right in Zoe's ear, Coco could tell Zoe all sorts of things – especially when she needed to add more sugar or when icing was clearly the wrong shade. Coco had saved Zoe's bacon – and her cakes – many times over. And she seemed to understand that she was strictly banned from being anywhere near the kitchen bench – cat hair definitely didn't belong in cakes.

'I've got a new order,' Zoe called out to Coco. 'A customer wants a castle cake for the fair on Sunday.'

Coco purred and stretched her front paws down the bookcase, clawing at book spines.

'Yes, yes, I know,' said Zoe, coming over to scratch the top of Coco's glossy brown head. 'I'm going to research castle cakes first. This has to be something special, Coco. Loads of people will see it. This is a big chance for Zinnia Jakes!'

Zoe put down the ScreenTouch, stood in front of the bookcase and began pulling out the most promising-looking books. But after several minutes of thumbing through dozens of pages, things weren't looking so sweet. Most of the castle cakes she found were for young children. They were made from ordinary old butter cake, which wasn't very exciting. Lots of them used upside down ice cream cones for towers, which made Zoe shake her head. All of the cakes were covered in icing, most of it pastel pink.

'Nothing looks like an authentic medieval castle, Coco,' said Zoe, screwing up her nose. 'And none of them are crumbly either.'

Coco jumped down onto Zoe's shoulder. She pawed at a ragged book on the middle shelf.

Zoe glanced up at Coco, then reached out and stroked the spine with her thumb. Coco had chosen a book that used to be

Zoe's mum's. Her name was signed in elegant letters on the first page, along with a list of the famous restaurants she had worked for as a pastry chef. Zoe read the title – *The History of Cake, Volume I.*

'I don't think that's going to help …' she began.

Then something flared into her mind. *I'm a medieval history professor*, the email had said. Zoe opened the book and scanned the contents page. There was one page on medieval cakes. She flipped to it. It said:

Medieval cakes were more like sweet loaves of bread than the special treats we eat today. Common ingredients were oats, honey, seeds, fruit and spices.

Zoe brightened. Honey sounded good. She had made a wonderful honey-flavoured teddy-bear cake for the Harrison twins just last month. She closed her eyes and imagined a tall cake covered in rough grey icing to resemble stones. With no ice cream cones in sight. She snapped the book shut. 'Perfect! That's what I'll do, Coco! I'll write to the professor to accept the job.'

She opened the ScreenTouch, balanced it on one knee and started typing. Coco shifted her weight on Zoe's shoulder. She was still for several moments and began to feel uncomfortably heavy, like a giant bag of flour. Then she meowed and leapt back onto the top of the bookcase. She turned her back to Zoe and dangled her tail over the edge, curling the tip slightly like a silken question mark.

Zoe sighed. 'Don't you like the sound of honey cake?'

Coco rolled her eyes.

'Why not?' asked Zoe.

But Coco didn't appear to be listening. Instead, she was swaying her body and tapping her paws. Her tail started snaking from side to side and her whiskers were quivering. Zoe stared at her.

'What are you doing, Coco?' She realised that Jam and Ben were playing a slow and heavy kind of tune, but it was very loud! 'Do you like medieval music?'

Coco stopped suddenly, melted onto her side and placed her front paws on her ears.

Zoe laughed. 'Okay, so you don't like the music!'

She finished typing her response and hit send. Then she grabbed her chocolate sprinkles notebook and began sketching some designs. She was sure that honey cake was correct for this job. Coco couldn't be right about everything.

Chapter 5

Zoe kept working on her designs until Ben and Jam's rehearsal had finished and Aunty Jam had started on dinner. Nina replied just as Zoe was setting the table.

Hi again, Zinnia!

I'm so excited that you can make a crumbling castle! A 12 o'clock delivery time on Sunday sounds brilliant, thank you. Your price for the cake is fine and I've sent the money to your bank account. I've decided to raffle the castle at the fair, so one lucky person will take home a Zinnia Jakes cake at the end of the day! I'm going to donate the raffle money to a charity I set up recently. The money will help to send disadvantaged children on fun camps and outings.

Nina

PS I've attached a map of the showground with an 'x' that shows my stall.

PPS Here I am with some of the children who were helped by our charity.

Zoe clicked on the attachment of the map and downloaded it. The other attachment was a photograph of a thrilled-looking woman standing with a small group of boys and girls.

Zoe smiled. She loved making cakes for good people and Nina definitely seemed like one of those.

A few minutes later, Jam put bowls of hot pasta on the table. Zoe showed her the emails and told her about the honey cake idea. Jam didn't say anything for a moment. She tapped her fingers on the table in a slow, steady rhythm.

'Honey cake sounds delicious, Zo, but …'

Zoe groaned. 'Not you too!'

'Well, there's this word here,' said Jam, pointing to Nina's first email. 'Authentic means true or real. It means your cake should be as medieval as you can make it. Remember, Nina's an expert on the time period.'

'But it will be medieval,' said Zoe. She held out the multi-coloured design she'd scratched onto her ideas notepad. 'See?' She was especially proud of the narrow windows in the towers. She'd recently seen them in a photograph of a famous Scottish castle with a long name that she kept forgetting.

'It looks the part, but I wouldn't have thought that medieval bakers used icing,' said Jam, reaching for the salad tongs.

'They didn't,' said Zoe. She pouted. 'But how else can I make the cake look like crumbling stone?'

'I'm not sure, but perhaps you should think about it a bit more,' said Jam. She twisted her hair around her fingers. 'When your mum first started, it sometimes took weeks for her to come up with a new creation. That's one reason she became such a brilliant chef.'

'But I've only got two days left!' squeaked Zoe.

Jam smiled and patted Zoe's knee. 'I just know you'll think of something wonderful.' She sighed. 'I wish I could think of something wonderful to improve the music we're playing. I don't think the crowd will like the medieval tunes the organiser has chosen. And Ben and I really need to attract some new fans from this performance.'

'Hmm,' said Zoe. She chewed on a piece of pasta. Her mind was filled with the cake-covering problem.

After dinner was cleared away, Zoe went to the computer with Jam and stared at page after page of castle images until her eyes felt as dry as cracker crumbs. To her growing annoyance, Coco seemed to be hinting that she should create the most complicated-looking castles that appeared on the screen. She tapped her paw on all the ones with difficult shapes, textures and colours. When Zoe ignored her, Coco swished her tail in her face and started walking across the keyboard. In the end, Zoe just glared at her. Coco put her nose in the air, went back to her bookcase and curled up in a ball.

By the time Zoe went to bed, she was in despair. She hadn't thought of anything else. Coco and Jam were right – she couldn't cover the cake with icing. She wouldn't even be able to use the very un-medieval chocolate rocks she had planned for a pathway. But what could she do that was authentic? Medieval baking seemed too plain and simple for making an eye-catching castle. Her shoulders slumped. Why on earth did she ever take on this job?

Chapter 6

Zoe woke the next morning with a start. Coco was patting her on the face with an ice-cold paw.

Zoe reached forward to tickle her ears. 'I have to start on the cake today,' she said. 'Or it won't be done in time.'

She flopped back onto her pillow. She had hoped she might have dreamt up some fabulous idea overnight, but her mind just felt cloudy and dull. And the faint scent of an idea was whispering at her – *give up altogether*. She squeezed her eyes shut. A picture floated into her mind … the group of children in Nina's photo. If the castle cake was raffled, the money could help a child. Even if it was only in a very bite-size way.

But could she really do it? She opened her eyes. Her gaze fell on her ScreenTouch, lying on her desk. Of course! She went over and touched the phone icon. She tapped on it and crossed her fingers. She wasn't sure what time it was in northern China …

A hairy face appeared on the screen. 'Zoe?'

'Dad!'

'What's up, love?' He was whispering and looked nervous under his fake beard.

'Oh, Dad, I'm having so many problems. I can't work out what to make for my new client. She wants an authentic medieval cake and I'm super stuck.'

'Authentic, hey? Sounds like a challenge.' Zoe had to strain to hear him. There were clanging sounds in the background and lots of loud voices.

'Dad, where are you?'

'I'm sneaking a peek in the kitchen of this restaurant as part of my review. I'm behind a vegetable bin.'

'Oh.'

'Zo, I know you've got this. Challenges can bring out your best. Your mum always used to say that.'

One of the background voices started bellowing. Dad glanced anxiously over his shoulder. 'The chef isn't happy with the soup. Anyway … you know what I think you should do about your cake? Try to relax for a moment. Sometimes you can't force an idea. Especially when it comes to fabulous cakes.'

'Well, okay. I'll try.' She struggled to smile.

'When I get stuck with my writing, I start reading articles by food writers I admire to trigger new ideas.' He lowered his voice. 'The chef here needs to simplify his dishes. He should be re-reading the traditional soup recipe – he's used too many herbs and spices. Cloves! Pepper! Ginger! Ridiculous.' He shook his head.

There was a particularly loud bang and the picture of Dad's face did a violent cartwheel. Then the image flipped back to normal.

Dad's next words were so soft that Zoe had to put her ear close to the ScreenTouch to hear them. 'That was close. I'd better get out of here. Hang in there, Zo. Zinnia Jakes has never failed. You are just as talented as Mum was. I believe in you.'

Zoe felt a warm glow. 'Thanks, Dad.'

'I'd better go. Good luck!'

Zoe tapped the screen to hang up and straightened her shoulders. Dad always made her feel better. And he was right.

Zinnia Jakes had never failed, and she wasn't about to now! There was still time.

She pulled on her watermelon slippers, picked up the ScreenTouch and went straight to the Zinnia kitchen. She sat on a stool and gobbled a slice of bread with peanut butter and drank a glass of orange juice. Mum had always said that pastry chefs needed to fill their tummies before they could make their best creations.

Once Zoe was done, she stood in front of the bookcase with Coco in her arms. If Dad was right, she needed to start from the beginning by going back to her recipe books. Although she didn't think there could be anything in them she hadn't seen already.

She sniffed the air. Jam must have got up early to practise because Zoe could smell one of her aunt's candles burning. It was orange. Jam said it helped with creativity.

Then Zoe heard the sound of the vielle begin. The tune sounded as thick as banana muffin batter to Zoe's ears. But Coco climbed out of Zoe's lap and gently began shuffling her paws in time to the beat. Then she stalked in front of the bookcase, stretched up and patted the spine of a book. Zoe pulled it out. It was the same volume of *The History of Cake* she had read before.

'I've already read this one, Coco,' she said with a sigh.

Coco flicked open the book with her claws and flipped it to the medieval page. Zoe pushed back her plaits and scanned it again. This time, she noticed a tiny caption at the bottom of the page.

Fruit cakes and gingerbread cakes were often eaten in early medieval times.

'Ginger!' she yelled, right next to Coco's ear.

Coco sprang into the air. All the fur on

her back and tail puffed up, making her look like a kind of mad squirrel.

'Sorry, Coco!' shouted Zoe. 'But I have an idea!'

Now she knew exactly what to do. She reached out for another recipe book, checked the index and flipped to page 354. There it was. *Medieval gingerbread*. She remembered it now. Her face softened. She had once helped her mother to make it, wrapped in an apron that was far too big for her. She had just started kindergarten. Zoe could still smell the spices that had warmed the air. Medieval gingerbread wasn't like modern gingerbread. There were only four main ingredients – honey, ginger, ground cloves and breadcrumbs.

A new image sifted into Zoe's mind. She didn't have to bake a solid cake. Instead, she could *build* the castle, brick by brick. Bricks made from medieval gingerbread would look crumbly and textured, just like those on the ancient castles she had been looking at. Perfect!

Zoe scrambled to the pantry. Everything seemed to be there. She snatched up her mum's old lavender apron. Then she hesitated. Something was missing. And only one person could help … Addie! She needed her fast. She grabbed the house phone and dialled.

'What do you mean, Zoe? How can you *build* a cake?' Addie sounded out of breath. When her mum had answered the phone, she'd said that Addie had got up bright and early to practise her tumbling act.

Zoe shook her head impatiently. 'Addie, could you please come over? I need help with some calculations.'

'Sure!' said Addie. 'Hold on, I'll check with Mum.'

Zoe heard a brief muffled conversation,

then Addie came back on.

'Mum says I can, but just for a short while. I need to get back to finish off my catapult and then I've got my last practice session with my gym team.'

'Great, thanks!' said Zoe.

She hung up and started to do some serious thinking. She decided how high she wanted the castle to be – it should reach just over her head. Zoe reckoned this would be low enough so it wouldn't wobble and tall enough to look like an imposing fortress.

Addie burst in a few minutes later, wearing her gymnastics gear. She was panting and fanning her face with her cap. She must have run the entire way to have made it so quickly. She guzzled down a glass of water while Zoe explained her idea as fast as she could.

'I'd like six towers and three turrets, with narrow windows in each one. Plus a double row of bricks around the castle to make a moat.' She danced from one foot to the other as the gingerbread castle came to life in her head. 'Oh, and you know those chocolate bricks I use for making ganache?'

Addie put down her glass and nodded. 'You mean the ones in the orange packet?'

'Yep. If I made gingerbread bricks about the same size, how many do you think I might need? I've made a guess but I'm not sure it's right. Here's a picture of the design ...' She tapped her ScreenTouch.

Addie studied the image that popped up and a smile spread across her face.

'Amazing!' she cried. 'Using bricks to make it is the best idea ever, Zo. It'll take me a while to do the calculations but I'll start right now.' She reached into her jacket pocket and pulled out a notebook.

'That's awesome, Ads! Thanks!' said Zoe.

She coaxed Coco up onto the bookshelf

and washed her hands. Now she was ready to begin. Jars of honey first. There were ten of them in the pantry. Five should do, she thought, reaching out for them. She opened the cupboard under the stove and pulled out her biggest saucepan. Then she began to gently heat the honey on the middle burner.

Coco was watching with a quizzical look on her face. But she was purring too.

'I've got to heat the honey until it boils,' Zoe said, scanning the recipe. 'Then we'll see a white foam.'

Coco wrinkled her nose and stopped purring.

Zoe giggled. 'Sounds gross, doesn't it? But it's okay. It's just what happens when the honey gets warm.' She kept stirring.

Within minutes, a white foam had started to form on the top of the honey. Addie set down her notebook and came over to peek into the saucepan. Together, they watched for the right moment to skim off the top. But they hardly needed to worry about that – when it looked and smelt like perfection, Coco stood up and shook herself. No need for an oven timer! The girls grinned at each other as Zoe pulled out a large metal spoon from her lime green utensils tin. She delicately scooped off the foamy top. Then Addie helped her weigh the correct amount of breadcrumbs. Zoe tipped them in along with the spices and stirred gently. Before long, a mouthwatering aroma filled the kitchen.

'Smells delicious!' called Addie, madly scribbling in her notebook again.

Zoe beamed. Getting started had been so difficult and now it was working beautifully. It was actually going to be ready in plenty of time. She wiped her hands on her apron. She had a pleasant feeling in her stomach, as warm and soothing as the heated honey.

Addie glanced at her watch. 'I'd better get going,' she said, sliding her notebook back into her pocket. 'I haven't quite finished but I'll call you with an exact number as soon as I can.' She frowned. 'You'll definitely need to make a few more bricks than you thought, though.'

'A few more is fine!' said Zoe. 'Great work, Addie!'

Zoe walked her to the front door and then dashed back to the kitchen. She began to wash her sticky hands. An email alert sounded and she turned her head. She had left her ScreenTouch on the bookshelf.

'Could you take a look, Coco?' she asked.

She could never quite believe that Coco could read, but Zoe often saw her peering at recipes. Afterwards, she would meow when Zoe pulled each correct ingredient from the pantry.

Coco moved closer to the screen.

'It is a new order?' asked Zoe, with one eye on the mixing bowl.

Coco moved her head from side to side.

'Is it Nina?'

Coco nodded.

'I wonder what she wants,' said Zoe. 'Maybe an earlier delivery time or something.'

Coco nodded again, her golden eyes shining.

'Well, that would probably be okay. This is much easier than I thought it would be, Coco. But let's see how we get on.' She beamed and turned her full attention back to the gingerbread mixture.

When she thought about it later on, Zoe couldn't quite believe how quickly her serene kitchen turned into a complete disaster zone.

Chapter 7

Zoe hummed to herself as she put the hot gingerbread mixture into the row of foil-lined tins. Like a proper medieval cook, she had not baked the gingerbread. Instead, it had been mixed and heated in the saucepan and now it needed to sit on the bench to cool.

Once the mixture was cooler, she began to press it all down with her hands. She heard Jam come into the kitchen when she was halfway through.

'Do you like this?' Jam asked.

Zoe turned and caught her breath.

Her aunt looked amazing – she was wearing a dark purple velvet dress that fell in graceful folds all the way to the floor.

'That's beautiful!' said Zoe. 'Where did you get it from?'

'The owner of the vielle, Abigail, lent it to me,' said Jam. 'She played at a medieval wedding recently.' She twirled around. 'You don't think it's too much for the fair?'

'Definitely not,' said Zoe. She imagined Jam playing the golden vielle with the dress creating a gorgeous backdrop behind it. 'It's scrumptious! Just like blueberry ice cream.'

Jam smiled. She gave Zoe a hug then stopped to scratch Coco under the chin. She was sitting right by Zoe's ScreenTouch. Jam looked at it curiously. 'Are you going to deliver the castle cake early?' she said.

'What?' said Zoe, wiping her hands on a tea towel.

'You've agreed to deliver it at 9 a.m., not

12 noon,' said Jam.

'No, I haven't,' said Zoe, puzzled.

'But that's what this email says,' said Jam. She leaned in towards the screen. 'Oh, wait a moment. The message hasn't gone yet. You must have typed it and then not hit send. Do you really want to deliver it so early? I thought you needed all the time you could get.'

'Jam, I haven't been near the ScreenTouch for hours,' said Zoe. What was going on? Her gaze fell on Coco, who was lazily using her claws to carve marks into the bookshelf.

Zoe's mind whirled. It wasn't possible, was it?

'Coco,' she said slowly. 'Where did you learn how to type?'

Coco's ears pricked up and she backed away towards the wall.

Zoe gasped. 'Coco, when I said it would probably be okay for me to deliver the cake early, I didn't mean you should reply to this email! Thank goodness you hadn't hit send yet!' She headed over to the ScreenTouch.

Coco appeared to sense trouble, because, in a flash, she jumped to the floor. Just at that moment, Zoe tripped over Jam's long skirt, causing them both to crash onto the tiles. Zoe fell painfully onto one knee and squealed. Coco yowled in fright and scampered past the bench, stepping in droplets of spilled honey. She shook her legs violently, pivoted on her toes, dashed forward and leapt wildly, sailing through the air towards the bookshelf.

'No!' called Zoe, trying to crawl using two hands and her good knee. 'Watch out for the ScreenTouch, Coco!'

Coco's eyes widened and she immediately twisted her body. But it was too late. Her front paws landed smack in the middle of the screen. Zoe rolled her eyes and Coco quickly did a frog-like spring to the other end of the bookshelf. She lay on her side and began frantically licking her paws.

'Are you all right?' said Jam, untangling herself from Zoe.

Zoe grimaced. 'Fine ... you?'

'I'm okay.' She tutted. 'Just a small rip in Abigail's dress. I'll have to mend it.' She got to her feet and hauled up Zoe as well. 'Thank goodness Coco didn't break anything or get near the gingerbread. But your ScreenTouch will need a good wipe.'

'Hmm.' Zoe limped over. The screen had a pair of sticky pawprints on it, glinting prettily in the light. She turned and gave Coco a look. Then she bent forward to take a look at the mysterious email. She felt her face turn milk-white under her freckles.

'Jam,' she whispered. 'The email! It's been sent! Coco must have accidentally hit the send button when she landed on the screen.'

The phone rang right next to her and Zoe robotically picked it up.

'Zoe? I've worked out how many bricks you need,' said Addie. 'It's a lot more than I thought. Those towers you've planned are so huge! You were actually about two hundred bricks short. That's not a problem, is it?'

Zoe didn't answer. She was gawping at the ScreenTouch with glazed eyes. A new message had popped up.

I'm thrilled you can deliver the cake early, Zinnia. I'll write a great review to tell everyone about it. Can't wait for tomorrow morning! Cheers,

Nina

Chapter 8

At 6 a.m. the next morning, Zoe sat limply on the kitchen stool, dabbing her forehead with a tea towel. She needed a few minutes' break. With Jam's help, she'd made all the gingerbread bricks – eight hundred of them – until late the night before. She had gone to sleep way past midnight and got up bright and early. The sun hadn't risen yet. She had honey stuck all over her Turkish delight sandals, flour in her hair and spices under her fingernails. She was starting to feel a faint sprinkle of hope now. She tasted a couple of the gingerbread bricks that had cooled down in the loaf tin.

'Marvellously soft and spicy!' said Zoe, feeling excited. They were so good she'd almost forgiven Coco for accidentally emailing Nina. Although it would be a while before Coco would be getting her favourite tuna biscuits again!

Zoe had also been busy with other things. When Jam got out the sewing kit to mend her dress, Zoe had spied some scraps of scarlet material and had used it to cut out tiny flags. In between practising her music, Jam had helped Zoe glue the flags onto toothpicks to decorate the turrets. Now Zoe had to come up with an idea for the moat. She wanted it to be a nice murky green. Normally she would just have made green icing. But she couldn't do that this time. It wasn't medieval. She was looking around in desperation when she spotted

Jam's herb garden out of the window. The leaves were waving in the breeze.

'Mint leaves,' she'd said aloud. 'I wonder ...'

If the leaves were arranged in a criss-cross pattern, they could look like rippling mossy water, she thought. But was mint grown in medieval times? She'd scrambled to check in *The History of Cake*, hardly daring to look. But she had soon pumped her fist in the air.

'Yes!'

Mint *had* been used in cooking and medicines. *Medieval people even scattered mint leaves on their floors to make a kind of air freshener*, Zoe read. She had skipped outside to grab several handfuls. Peppermint and ginger together would be a medieval scent sensation!

Last of all, Zoe had made a simple honey sauce to stick the bricks together. The sauce had dried fruit, vinegar and olive oil in it, along with the honey. These were all authentic medieval ingredients.

Zoe wearily got to her feet. It was now 7.30 a.m. and everything was ready to build the castle. The doorbell rang. It was Addie, so things felt even better. Although Zoe wished she would stop talking …

'… And then we do three forward flips and a backbend'.'

Zoe glanced up with a frown.

Addie's hands were on her hips. 'Zoe, are you listening to me?'

'Yep, yep, yep,' said Zoe. The clock was ticking. She took a deep breath. She needed Addie's mathematical eye to build nice straight walls.

'Actually, Addie,' she said. 'I really need your help, please.'

'All right,' Addie said, 'what do you need me to do?'

'Build!' said Zoe, spreading out her

plan like a fresh sheet of baking paper. She showed Addie where the base layer of bricks needed to go on the cake board. Then they set to work, building the bricks higher and higher, painting on honey sauce as they went. Addie stopped Zoe now and again to remind her to leave gaps for the windows.

Jam came in when Zoe had just finished filling the moat with mint leaves. She was wearing her beautiful gown, along with a headdress – a silky violet circlet with a dark purple veil. She looked exactly like a princess from medieval times.

'I'm going to start packing Beethoven with the music gear,' she said, her skirt sweeping the floor as she walked. 'I'll try to leave space for you girls.' She smiled. 'The castle is wonderful.' She peered into the tub that Addie had brought with her. 'Oh, wow! Did you make this catapult and the dragon too?'

'Yes, I did,' beamed Addie. 'I made the dragon for the catapult to fling. I'll get extra points for that.'

'It's so clever. Isn't it, Zoe?'

'It's great,' said Zoe, still focused on the cake. 'Addie has fantastic ideas!'

While Jam started loading Beethoven, Zoe stood on tiptoes and placed the flags on the turrets. She wiped her sticky hands on her apron and stepped back.

'Something is missing, but I'm not sure what ...' Zoe said, chewing her lip.

Then a thought struck her and she ran to her spice rack. She selected 'Dried Mint' and carefully sprinkled it around the edges of her castle. She clapped in delight. Now the cake board had become the grassy hill she had first imagined.

She studied the whole creation. The castle looked strong and bold. Zoe could imagine elegant lords and ladies in velvet cloaks living inside. A crumbled gingerbread pathway drew her eye to the moat, with its gentle, minty waves. The flags seemed to be fluttering. There was even a drawbridge, made of gingerbread bricks stuck together. Zoe had carefully poked holes at the edges, tied on string and placed it on the front of the castle. Behind it was a gingerbread portcullis, a type of criss-cross gate.

Zoe breathed in the castle's spicy scent. It was tinged with a hint of peppermint. 'What do you think?' she asked Addie.

'It's fantastic!' she said, nodding enthusiastically. She glanced at her watch. 'And just in time too. We have to leave in five minutes.'

'Five minutes?' Zoe screeched. 'Help me with the box, please, Addie!'

Addie was already heading to the hall cupboard. Quickly, Zoe snatched up her

ScreenTouch and snapped a picture of the cake. Then she sent it in a message to Dad. He replied instantly: *It looks incredible, Zo! So proud of you!*

Zoe smiled. She and Addie gently picked up the castle and placed it inside the Zinnia Jakes box. Addie had picked the very tallest one and the cake fitted perfectly. She expertly folded the top while Zoe raced to the laundry cupboard to get Coco's cat carrier. Coco glared from the top of the bookcase and swished her tail wildly.

'I know, I know,' said Zoe. 'But if you want to come with us then you have to get in.' She reached up and hauled her down. Then she gently placed her into the carrier, making sure her tail was well inside before she fastened the clips. Zoe ripped off her apron and rubbed her sweaty palms on her candy-stripe overalls.

'Girls?' called Jam. 'We need to go.

It's taken me a while to get Beethoven started and I don't want to stop the engine. Hurry now!'

Chapter 9

Zoe raced to the kitchen bench and scooped up the cake box with both arms. Addie grabbed Coco's carrier and balanced her tub on the top. She darted through the front door, with Zoe on her heels.

Beethoven was rumbling in the driveway. Clouds of black smoke were coming from the exhaust pipe and the smell of horribly burnt sugar seared Zoe's nostrils. She held her breath as she flew past.

Jam opened the rear door for Addie and she scrambled in. On the very back seats were the vielle case, Jam's amplifier and microphones, and lots of cords, cables and music stands. Zoe slid into the front seat with the cake box. The top of the box grazed the ceiling as she got in. Zoe gritted her teeth. But there was no time to check the cake. Jam reached over and put on Zoe's seatbelt.

'Ready, Addie?' Jam said over her shoulder.

'Yes!' she said. Her voice was slightly muffled. Zoe could hear Coco hiss from inside her carrier.

'Sorry, Coco. We'll be there soon!' she called.

Jam pressed on the accelerator and the engine roared, then spluttered and coughed. The van wobbled like a giant jelly. Then it stopped.

'Oh no, please don't, Beethoven!' said Jam. She turned the key again. Zoe's heart thumped. The engine spluttered once more, but this time it kept going.

'Thank goodness!' breathed Zoe. 'Let's go!'

They rattled off down the street and lurched to the right. Zoe knew that the showground was only ten minutes away but she wasn't sure how close it was to 9 o'clock. At least they were on their way. The ride was so rough that Zoe had to grab onto the dashboard with one sweaty hand. She propped the cake box against her chest, holding it there with her other hand. She winced at every bump and jolt.

A few shuddery turns later, Zoe saw the sign for the showground in the distance. The leafy road leading up to the gates was usually quite empty, but today it was lined with cars and crowds of people.

'Okay,' said Jam, as Beethoven rasped up to the iron gates, 'let's go over the delivery plan now. I've been given a special parking space, which is close to Nina's book stall. Zoe, you can slip out with the cake while Addie and I distract Nina. Then—'

CLUNK! Beethoven shuddered twice and stopped dead.

Zoe's eyes widened. Her fingers stiffened on the cake box. She watched Jam twist the key.

'Come on, Beethoven,' Jam pleaded.

There was a terrible grinding sound from the engine. People passing by abruptly stepped away.

'That's not good,' muttered Jam. She tried the key again, but this time nothing at all happened. She reached down and picked up her phone.

'I'll call Ben. He should be on his way here. We can squeeze the music gear into his car. But there won't be room for you two.' She tapped on the screen and put the phone to her ear.

'We'll have to take the cake on foot,' said Zoe, turning her body to hide the cake box from a passer-by. 'And we have to go now. Zinnia Jakes is never late!'

She swivelled around to face Addie, who was staring at her watch. 'Only ten minutes left!' she wailed. A frown was creasing her forehead. 'We can't walk with the cake, Zoe. There's no way to hide the Zinnia box.'

'It's okay, Addie,' Zoe said. 'I think I have an idea.'

Chapter 10

'Bye!' said Jam into her phone. She tapped on the screen and turned to Zoe. 'Okay. Ben's almost here.'

Zoe was staring at her aunt. Jam's purple veil was long … very long. 'Aunty Jam,' she said, 'I need your veil.'

Jam looked puzzled.

'To put over the Zinnia box,' said Zoe. 'It will hide it perfectly.'

Addie had already jumped out of Beethoven, clutching her tub, and had opened Zoe's door. Zoe waited for a group of girls to pass by, then she took the veil from Jam. Just before Zoe draped it over, she remembered about the box scraping on Beethoven's ceiling. She really needed to check it. Carefully, she unfolded the box top and peered in.

'Oh no!' she whimpered. Three bricks from the top of the high turret had tumbled off. She blinked and tried to think clearly. There was no time to panic! An image formed in her mind. One of the castle cakes she'd seen in her recipe books had dragons perching on its turrets. She could just imagine a dragon swooping down onto a medieval castle and knocking off some of the stones.

Zoe looked pleadingly at Addie. 'Do you think I could have your dragon?'

'But ...' Addie swallowed. She hesitated for a moment, then opened the tub and gave Zoe the dragon.

'Thank you, Ads. You're the best!' said

Zoe, pushing the dragon into the soft gingerbread bricks. 'Can you help me fix the box top again? I'll get Coco.'

Addie nodded.

'Here's Ben,' said Jam, shading her eyes. 'You'd better go. Good luck, girls!'

Zoe twisted around and opened the cat carrier. Coco sauntered out of the van and leapt onto Zoe's shoulder. The girls headed for the gates.

'Which way do we go?' asked Addie.

'Straight ahead,' said Zoe, pointing. She was half-running now. 'I printed out Nina's map last night. She is at Stall 16. Jam and Ben are playing in the grassy area behind it.' As she spoke, Ben's car drove past and tooted.

'My gymnastics display is at the same grassy area later on,' panted Addie. 'But my catapult has to be delivered to the McGregor Building … there it is!' She pointed to a brick building standing tall among the red and white awnings of the maze of stalls.

Addie slowed down and checked her watch. 'It's 8.52,' she said. 'My entry has to be in by 9.' She looked over at Zoe and took a deep breath. 'I'll help you first. There'll probably be time.'

Zoe looked at the beautiful creation inside Addie's tub. Through the clear lid, she could see all the fine details that Addie must have worked so hard to create. Addie was biting her lip.

Zoe shook her head. 'Don't be silly. You might miss out on entering your catapult.' She paused. 'It's important.'

'Are you sure?' said Addie.

'Of course,' said Zoe. 'Coco will help me. You go on.'

With a worried glance, Addie raced off.

Zoe charged onwards. 'I hope I make it,' she said softly to Coco. Coco rubbed her face against Zoe's cheek.

Just a few minutes to go. Where was Stall 16? Where? To her left, Zoe could see a lemonade stall labelled as Stall 12. Stall 13, *Ye Olde Shoes*, was next to it. Then up ahead, she saw Stall 16. Under the awning was a long white table covered in books with a castle on their front covers. A woman dressed in red was arranging them on the table. It was Nina! Perfect!

Or not so perfect, really, Zoe thought. There were people everywhere and Nina was glancing around every few moments. Her eyes were worried. Zoe's heart sank.

'What are we going to do?' she whispered to Coco.

Coco clamped her teeth onto Zoe's hair. She gently tugged, turning Zoe's head towards the grassy area. Ben had parked his car there. Jam had taken the vielle out of its case and was putting up the music stands while Ben, dressed in a tunic and a felt hat, was plugging in the amplifier and microphones. Zoe realised she hadn't even asked Jam what time she and Ben had to play. She felt a sour taste in her mouth. Jam had been so worried about this gig.

She watched as Jam and Ben sat down, nodded to each other, plucked a few strings and started playing their first tune. Zoe turned back to Stall 16. She hoped that Nina might magically leave or that the bunch of people near her might head over to Jam and Ben. But nothing like that happened.

'We've only got two choices, Coco,' Zoe whispered. 'We can deliver the cake and have everyone find out about Zinnia Jakes. Or we forget all about it and let down Nina.'

Zoe felt tears welling in her eyes and she furiously blinked them away.

Coco began kneading Zoe's shoulder with her front paws. Her claws prickled straight into Zoe's skin.

'Ow! Don't do that!' said Zoe. She looked up to tell her off. Coco's ears were twitching back and forth like pastry brushes. Exactly in time to Jam and Ben's music.

Zoe straightened, her eyes sparkling. 'Coco,' she said, 'I need your help!'

Chapter 11

Coco tilted her head and stared straight into Zoe's eyes.

'You can distract the crowd for me,' said Zoe. 'You just need to dance. You love dancing!'

Coco pulled back her whiskers.

'Please, Coco. You owe me one. Remember that little emailing problem you caused?' Coco shuffled her legs and looked at her toes.

Zoe turned back to Jam and Ben. There were dozens of people walking right past them. No-one was lingering. Jam and

Ben were glancing at each other with pinched faces.

'You'll be helping Jam and Ben too,' Zoe said to the top of Coco's head. 'They need this show to work. Pretty please? With a cherry on top?' She held her breath.

Coco raised her head and made a chattering sound in the back of her throat. She bounded onto the ground, then darted through the legs of the crowd. She charged straight into a flock of seagulls that were squabbling over some hot chips. They flew upwards in a squawking cloud. But Coco never bothered to chase wildlife. She streaked past them with her nose in the air, heading straight for Jam and Ben. For one horrified moment, Zoe wondered if Coco was going to jump onto Jam's lap and mess up her playing. But she slowed down as she got nearer and ambled the last few steps to Jam's feet. Then, like a swirl of hot chocolate sauce, she circled the vielle's spike, winding her tail around it. Jam looked startled and almost dropped her bow.

Then Coco began to dance.

She started with a graceful tail twist and twirled on the spot like a ballerina. She followed this with three forward somersaults. Then she was back on all fours, balancing on the very tips of her claws. She swayed her head from side to side, then sprang over Jam's microphone stand, landing on her front paws. Every movement was done precisely, exquisitely, in time to the music.

'Look at the kitty cat!' called a little boy on a man's shoulders. He pointed his dripping ice cream cone in Coco's direction. 'She's dancing!'

'She really is!' said a woman right near Zoe. 'That's amazing!'

People walking by began pressing

towards Jam and Ben. Zoe lost sight of Coco in the crowd, but then suddenly spotted her soaring into the air high above Ben's shoulder. She giggled.

'What's your cat's name?' called a voice.

'Coco,' said Jam, elegantly bowing the vielle.

'Go, Coco the cat!' yelled a man.

Some of the growing crowd began to clap in time to the music. Ben and Jam played faster and faster. Coco must have been keeping up because the cheers got louder and dozens of phones were held up high.

Zoe peered at Stall 16. Nina had moved to the edge of the stall. She was standing on a chair and craning her neck to see over the crowd.

'Great!' Zoe muttered to herself. It was now or never.

Swiftly, she moved to the other side of the stall and pushed the cake box onto the table with trembling hands. No-one was paying any attention. She whisked off the veil and stuffed it down the front of her overalls. Then she fished inside her pocket and prised out a striped tin. Inside was a red zinnia. Zoe laid it on top of the box and began to back away. Relief was flowing through her like melted butter.

Then a hand landed on her shoulder and almost made her scream.

Chapter 12

Zoe whirled around faster than an electric beater. 'Addie!'

'You did it!' Addie beamed. 'Great work, Zoe!' She gaped at the crowd. 'I didn't think Jam and Ben's music would be so popular.' She suddenly tipped back her head, looking up at the sky. 'Is that … Coco?'

Zoe grinned. 'Let's move a bit further away,' she said, 'so no-one sees us near the cake.' She grabbed Addie's hand. 'Did you make it on time?'

'I did!' said Addie, following Zoe a few steps away to a bread stall. 'There were some amazing entries from older kids though, so I don't think I'll win first place. Plus it would have got a better score if the catapult had ...' She stopped and shook her head. 'Never mind.'

'What do you mean?' said Zoe. Then she pressed her hands to her face. 'You would have got extra points if it had something to fling, wouldn't it? Your dragon ...' She hung her head. 'I'm so sorry, Addie.'

'It's okay, Zoe,' Addie whispered. 'That's what besties are for! Zinnia Jakes needed it more than I did.' She paused. 'I've got to get changed for the tumbling display. It's starting soon. You're going to watch, right?'

'Of course,' said Zoe, with a smile. 'Besties.'

Addie beamed and nodded. She bounded off towards the grassy area.

Jam and Ben had stopped playing and were talking to people in the crowd. Then there was a big whoosh in the air and Coco landed on Zoe's shoulder.

'There you are!' said Zoe. 'Clever girl.' She stroked Coco all the way from her head to the tip of her tail, just the way she liked it.

A woman's voice boomed out. 'Wow! It's unbelievable!'

Zoe turned. Nina had opened the front flaps of the cake box.

'Look at this!' she called out to the man in the next stall. She slid out the cake.

'That's impressive,' he said. 'I'll buy a ticket! Is it a Zinnia Jakes?'

'Yes,' said Nina, holding up the flower. 'I was starting to think it wouldn't arrive in time. But she's made it with one minute to spare. How on earth did she deliver it without me seeing her?'

The man shrugged. 'The same thing happened last year when we ordered a piano cake for my daughter. Must be magic!'

At that moment, a light breeze picked up. Some of the dried mint swirled up and floated around the castle like fairy dust.

Nina clasped her hands. 'Well, this cake is definitely magical,' she said, reaching out to touch one of the tiny flags. 'And medieval! It's made from gingerbread!' She picked up one of the fallen bricks and popped it in her mouth. She chewed for a moment and sighed. 'Truly authentic. And look at the mint leaves! Did you know that medieval people scattered their floors with them?'

Zoe hid a proud smile. She felt for Jam's veil in her overalls. She smoothed out the wrinkles with her fingers and walked towards her aunt, who was talking to a fan.

Zoe caught Jam's eye and applauded. Jam waved her bow high over her head and gave Zoe her brightest smile.

'Thank you!' said Zoe, as she carefully

placed the veil on the chair next to her aunt. Jam nodded.

Zoe glanced at her watch and rushed off to watch Addie's tumbling display. She loved every moment of it – and she felt a huge buzz when Addie's team won first prize. Right after the crowd finished their applause, there was an announcement over the loudspeaker. The results of the catapult competition! Zoe crossed her fingers.

'First place – Zac Fisher. Second place – Daisy Noonan. And third place … Addie Chen.'

Zoe clapped until her hands were sore. She felt so happy! Then there was a tug on her sleeve. A boy was gazing at Coco.

'Is she your cat? She's so cool! Can I get a photo?'

'Us too!' said a group of teenage girls on her other side.

'Your cat is incredible! We saw her dance

earlier,' said a woman walking past. 'She ought to be in the movies.'

'Did you teach her to move to music or is it natural?' asked the man with her.

'I … uh …' Zoe's eyes flicked from one face to the other. She twisted around to see Coco. She was sitting on her shoulder, licking her paw and cleaning her face with it.

'So let me get this straight,' Zoe whispered to Coco. 'Jam, Ben, Addie and I all work so hard getting ready for today, but you're the one who gets the adoring crowd. And you didn't put in any work at all! I mean, cats don't go to dancing lessons or music classes.' She laughed.

Coco paused for a moment, then tapped Zoe daintily on the nose with her paw.

Zoe peered at her with a big smile. 'They don't, do they?'

Coco purred loudly. Very loudly. Right in Zoe's ear.

Zinnia Jakes's Secret Recipe File:

Medieval Gingerbread

Hi everyone! Here is my secret recipe for medieval gingerbread. I hope you enjoy making it! And remember, baking should be infused with imagination, drizzled with determination and frosted with fun!

Note: Make sure you ask an adult to help with putting aside the ingredients and the baking, especially when you boil the honey.

★ You will need ★

- 250 ml honey
- 230 g fresh breadcrumbs
- 2 tsp ground ginger
- ½ tsp ground cloves
- 2 pinches of pepper
- A saucepan
- A spoon
- A loaf tin
- Baking paper

★ Instructions ★

1. First, heat the honey slowly in a saucepan. Bring it to the boil (that means lots of bubbles!) while you stir it. Use a wooden spoon to skim off any white foam you see on the top of the mixture. Don't worry about the foam - it's a good sign that things are working!

2. Stir the breadcrumbs into the honey. Take the saucepan off the heat. Be careful – it will be hot!

3. Add the ginger, ground cloves and pepper to the honey mixture and stir. Try not to sneeze!

4. Leave the mixture in the saucepan for a few minutes. When it's less hot, line a loaf tin with baking paper and press in the gingerbread with your fingertips. You'll love this bit – it feels soft and warm. Leave it to cool. Don't be tempted to try it yet.♥

5. When it is cold, cut it into bricks, or any other shape you like!

★ Yum! Bon appetit! ★

★ ABOUT THE AUTHOR ★

Brenda Gurr adores anything to do with spies, adventure and mysteries, so writing a book about someone with a secret identity is something she has always longed to do. Add to that her love of cats (she owns two magical Burmese cats) and her habit of baking far too many sweet treats, and you have all the ingredients for the world of Zinnia Jakes! A former storytelling fairy, drama teacher and school worksheet writer, Brenda is the author of numerous books for children. This is her first chapter book series.